FAITH ON GOD

A BUSINESS OPPORTUNITY

SAMARASAM SADASIVAM

To my family, friends and well wishers!

Contents

Acknowledgements

I would like to thank my friends who inspired me to start something, which made me to write this book.

Thank you all for being the part of my adventure. Your belief in me have made this a reality.

Thank you!
Samarasam

CHAPTER ONE

World Productivity Day

On World Productivity Day, Tuesday 20th June 2034.

An interview with **Mr. Maaran**, a successful entrepreneur owning multiple areas of business. He started his career as an IT professional developing python projects in a service-based company.

Very soon, he moved out of employee role and took the entrepreneur role starting with his own unique stuffs. He is also a best-selling author of *"You can't be Happy"*.

'Let's hear him from his own words.

Hello Sir, my name is Kilian. We feel very great to have you here and happy to interview you personally.

Hello Kilian. Nice to meet you!

Kilian: Shall we begin to listen your amazing story, sir?

CHAPTER TWO

The Inspiration

We all know you own multiple products, businesses and brands now. Could you please share what made you to jump from a software professional to here? What made you to take the decision to become an entrepreneur?

Maaran: My father was a Post Man. With all the constant salary and 30 years of his compounded savings and work, he built us a sweet small home at Dharmapuri. I got graduated by the time and it was 2 years later, I had applied a loan to purchase a land in Kelambakkam, Chennai. It was a tough decision for me to take a loan when I had just 2 years of experience in a company and was earning a low-decent package. I knew future will be tough, so I felt I should better start taking all the risks and new commitments when I'm younger.

At that time, there was a bad news and good news. There was a road expansion at my place. Our street was not a main road where businesses usually runs. It was in the middle of some nowhere area. We really don't know why that was happening and why the expansion was needed to our area. We still din't get the answer or understood it.

Many officials came and gave us notice. They did estimation for each house based on the govt rate and the estimated amount was not even half for the amount needed to replace the price of land and house. It was a brand new house and we just spent 2 years only, Yet we had many beautiful memories and I planned a lot in that home for future. They gave us 3 months of final notice, after a year of all the protests from my area.

It was that day, I was working casually, had tea breaks with friends, chit chats. I got a call from our landline at evening around 5 PM where we usually work productively. I took it and it was my dad with low voice "They demolished our house. You don't need to come now. Uncle helped us to move things".

You don't actually get my emotion when im talking in English. He said"veeta idichutanga pa, nee vara venaam; naanga pathukurom. Mama vanthu thingslaam move pannitaru."

That's all. I din't utter a word. Just sounded hmmmm. It was very painful. The pain was not about the demolition. I felt pain to digest how dad and mom would take that.

> *"For them it was everything. Their dream, hard work, savings, peace and hope on future."*

The officers always told us that the road expansion is to help the transport which will help lifting future growth of the state. There was a small temple in the same street just after 6 houses of ours. But not a even a single brick of the temple got broken. They made a curved extended road by demolishing only the residential homes. The temple was completely safe. I am not complaining about that.

> *"The good news is the realization of this world."*

The temple was safe and steady till now but many of us lost homes. They cared for the temple but didn't think of how much pain we were going through.

For the officials it was their duty, I understand, but they din't feel anything about us. They did not show humility when they were going to make us all sad. At-least they should have done that.

All those incidents signalled me on the *positive demands*which will last for ever until the last human in this world. If my house is under a temple, that could be the safest I felt. I can get free electricity, donations, I can open a shop just in front of that, *An ongoing everlasting business model*. And that's where I started to see all the potential businesses I could make.

CHAPTER THREE

Opportunities are in front of us!

Kilian: I'm so sorry for the miserable situation you and your family had experienced. Lets move on to the next one. What did you do after that? How that situation made you an entreprenuer?

I didn't quit my job. That was paying all our bills. But I got a loan for the land purchase and my father received some money from the government on the demolishing thing where we had our life's hope. We moved to a even smaller rented house. And my father gave the entire money he recived for the hourse to me.

My family is different in many ways. My father never advised me on putting all the money into savings account unlike his generation friends. So, I always look for investment options, the low risk and low return investments.

With my father's money, I got an engineer to build a small but different kind of temple in the land I purchased. Just for 1/3rd of the area only. Rest I left it to build a house in future.

The temple which I built had 3 important gods and I made sure it had different architecure so that it should not look like a temple which focuses on one main god.

One is "Dakshinamoorthy(an avatar of shiva) " better known for granting jobs or helping in any kind of tasks.

Second one is Lakshmi(Goddess of wealth) for whom I spent more money on statues, architectures, and decorations.

The third is Vinayaka who is mandatory and needed for any worshippers.

And few other gods at necessary places.

Now, the walls have great sayings, proverbs, Thirukkurals, wisdom words.

It was built in a way such that people can come and worship anytime. There is no person assigned for poojas. Its all self and people responsibility to keep in a line as instructed and constructed to help them to achieve that. Sayings like 'taking responsibility to clean temple once in a while will give good deed on your account' posted on walls. All the walls are pure white and oil and dust resistant ones.

The important one is Money Bank Boxes. There are many and each served different purposes. Kept one at each god. Kept one for donations next to a board saying the list of expenses needed to help people to do self-worship in a silent and cleaner way in this beautiful temple concept.

There is a board which had all the good things done to the society from the money taken from money boxes. The first one I did was, from my wallet I took money and provided stationary items, books to one poor girl and I advertised it there. I considered this as an investment. So, people would think that I am using temple money for a good purpose other than for maintenances.

There were boards which says "if you really missing the contribution for oil, milk, traditional lightings and stuffs like in the traditional temple, please donate at the Poor box which has a note "All of this will go to feed someone and you should be grateful to be a part of lifting and feeding someone. Thank you for your heartful contribution"

The walls had nice calendars to display important days and timings. So people don't miss visiting there.

One day, I somehow managed to bring a counsellor in that area to make him to give 5 cycles to the local students which was bought from the temple collections only. This was also some kind of investment i Intentionally made. The counsellor was very happy since he din't take a penny from his pocket, yet he looked like doing some social service to the society. That day was really a successful one. Many had visited the temple by seeing counsellor's arrival and all looked the beauty of the unique temple with wisdom thoughts on boards, spacious and stone chairs for elder people to spend time. Words like "**please allow elder ones to sit and be more kind**" attracted many young people.

Lots of new visitors started coming to spend meaningful time with this bright temple which have various things to see and distract ourselves into something new.

Later I brought solar lights all around temple and insisted people on the awareness of renewable energy. There are no single oil lamps at this temple till today. Yet people like this environment and feel like this is modern traditional. All the small lights are electric lamps and I made sure it smells like traditional temples. People might hate looking at electric lamps even though they are beautiful. But the nice smell surrounded all over the temple helped them feel better. Every corner and bit of the temple had scented stones, himalayan salt rocks and plenty of meidcinal plants with anti-insect purposes and also provided great smell to the environment.

Now you will understand how much amount of money I had invested just to bring the people, so they like spending time here and visit often.

But do you think, did I get all the invested money via those money boxes.

Definitely no. Not yet. It was a huge money I invested regularly other than the 'demolition compensation money'.

"But It did help me to start many more businesses using this temple."

CHAPTER FOUR

The more you look, the more you see!

Interviewer: OMG!

Yeah! Even till today, I am still researching what are all the new businesses I can start.

Parallelly, I made a simple android and iOS app. Not for this temple.

> *"To have temple for everyone at their own hands."*

The simple app I created provides these purposes.

1. It can set automatically set up some god's wallpaper.
2. Options to mark important days so that your preferred god wallpaper will appear on that day. Many people prefer to look at specific gods when they open their eyes in the morning.
3. Devotional ring tones.
4. Devotional play lists.
5. Study area with lots of articles to read on god's adventures, books and many more.
6. Meditation music.

7. Morning ritual music, specific to each different occasion or festival.
8. You can do digital poojas if you want.
9. Donations, pooja fee, and many more interesting stuffs.

And many more. I really put lots of effort to bring this perfect app. This doesn't hang up anytime.

This gave me all the money I invested on the temple architecture. Yes, within a month, it got 5 million downloads all over the world by our great worshippers.

I also collect data and sell. With the data collected from spending, account credit messages, location and frequency of repeated activities, "They are the professionals, educated ones, salaried ones are the most ones using this app"

It gives them what they want. I see many people start opening this app from railway station and it runs till they reach the destination. They carry their own temple within their pocket.

Daily during travel, before exams, before opening the office book, before and after lunch and right before sleep my app helps them to give some confidence by showing god's picture which will give them peace.

During my childhood, some of my friends always had some god's picture at their pockets.

My collegues had god's picture at their desks. Before exam results many wanted to go to temples. Some used to be nervous often and I wanted them to visit this temple or just to see some god's photo which gives hope to them.

> *"Like people say "God is everywhere" . So, God is in smartphones too by design and this philosophy."*

In better words " Thoonilum irupaar, thurumbilum irupaar" and in Mobile too now.

And I feel good that people get positive feelings while using this app.

CHAPTER FIVE

Multiple Products, Multiple Businesses

Kilian: Awesome Sir! I am becoming your fan and myself getting some ideas for my life.

Mr. Maaran, please tell us about your other business as well.

Yes sure. The temple I said right. It's a path to lots of other opportunities. Especially small businesses.

We all see there are plenty of shops near each temple. Some are selling worship related items. Some focus on toys. Some with snacks & foods.

What I picked is flower business. Only the jasmines and there are many type of it. I had a friend who's family is cultivating jaathi-mullai, one of the costly kind compared to other jasmines.

They sold 1kg of flowers for 120 rupee only which was at 2021 any day any occasion. If we buy in local shops during any festive days, we cannot get 50 grams for 100 rupee. That sparked another small business where I initially put a metal shed container in front of our temple and I employed a person who sold jasmines earlier. But this time, he gets monthly salary and all the profit comes to me. Me and my friend looked over how to transport flowers like any other big business man do that all over India. And we started transporting from Ooty ground to Dharmapuri.

The flower demand is always there. And based on the demand I would import more and more. And on normal days, I would just take few kgs only.

And I sell them in *nice packets.* Selling wholesale on festive and mukurtham/marriage days with higher rate.

Supplying to decorative consultants too now.

Neighbours send SMS to book flower boxes advance.

I have many branches now all over the district and each with a different name for a purpose.

CHAPTER SIX

Attractive things attracts people

Same way, I started another model to sell items needed for holy things. I would say this as holy market.

I sell pumpkins used for ceremonies and other events.

Coconuts only for temple, occasions, functions and marriages.

And all the items you need for any kind of occasion. Housewarming, marriages, poojas, temple visit, land registration, water boring and many more.

But I felt some competition in the beginning. Later I found better ways to sell.

I introduced *the packages*.

Package for

- Housewarming ceremony
- Festive poojas
- Temple marriages
- Marriage
- And others.

So, the boxes kept in store will have the package name and the list of items to put inside. So, anyone who works on the store doesn't need to worry about knowing the occasion. He just need to read on the list pasted on everybox and fills them. Like everyone else, the price varies based on the demand or on important business days. Business days mean, all the muhurtham & festive days.

We also started selling these stuffs at wholesale to all the shops near some famous temples. Temples have too many different shops and I don't compete with the ones who sell vessels, toys, fancy shops, snacks & clothing. We just concentrate on the stuffs used for **holy purposes** like poojas and ceremonies.

My shop replaced few shops in a famous temple at Mailam near Dindivanam. But we employed most of those who lost at my newly bought 7 acres of land where I cultivate Lotus in pools, arugampull(holy grass), dwarf coconut trees and few others too.

CHAPTER SEVEN

Tips for Business

Kilian: Please give us few tips for us, sir!
Maaran: Ofcourse!

1. People don't always want to buy something all time. It is triggered when they see the products. So, when you make something or want to sell, we must know **how to make the people see our products**.

2. You can sell anything you want this world. But you can only do at the right place and to the right people. You no need to cultivate grass (Arugam-pul). It's always free if you are ready to look around. You can sell them at festive season or at any temple right on right day? So always **choose right customers for right products and at right occasion**. And you can sell anything.

3. This one is about storing the valuables.

   a. For the last 15 years, we are seeing M-sand, P-sand for constructions. Because there is no white sand anymore left to take from dead rivers. Or govt have strict rules to not touch the river sand anymore. But few of my friends who has large mills and sheds, bought huge amount of white sand long before and they dint use it till now. So, in future some people might be interested to get that fine sand at a greater price if you have it already bought legally and stored.

b. Few people buy and accumulate silver. Silver is not just a precious metal. It is an industrial purpose metal. Industries need silver to make solar panels and for other energy production methods. When we go towards renewable energy source more and more, silver will be in demand and there is a potential to sell. And they can't bargain while buying; they have to buy at market price. **Store it to sell in future**

4. **If you are just a maker, you may not get more profits.** Only the personor broker who buys from the maker and sells it to end customers are the ones who take big profits. Ethically, we hurt the makers by not sharing some of our profits. ***But if you have the potential to do both making and selling, then you will be at the TOP 1%.*** That's why, the corporate companies started buying lands and started cultivating their own products and sell at their stores now. Earlier also, they were getting huge profits by buying products from farmers and selling at their stores. Now when they started making their own products, they cut many expenses and make huge money.

You know Bill Gates is the America's Top Farmland Owner. Guess, you got the point!

The point is you start producing something small if you can and sell them.

For the immediate profits, go for buying and selling at high. There's no doubt on that method.

CHAPTER EIGHT

The guts

Thank you so much Sir, for all the ideas. It is really inspiring.

On what Faith, you started all of these your unique products and unique approach?

> *"5000 years later, there will be too much demand for food products and agriculture.*
>
> *And I strongly believe that, **your great great grandson, will break a pumpkin at a high-tech road in front of his newly constructed home.** "*

You should see, **billion-dollar rocket launches gets rituals of pumpkin breaking.**

People don't eat the things, the nature provided gold, and it will be same until the last person to see the earth.

So, after 5000 years, my company would evolve by having some Agri research company to make these pumpkins using modern tissue culture, will make*artificial milk for 'temple rituals and cinema poster'* and will supply the products from housewarming to billion dollar rocket launches.

Our company will produce Agri products not for eating, **but for breaking on the land and road for rituals.**

If you build some home in Mars, do not forget to get a holy-product package from us at a best rate in a best-looking partitioned box and we will door deliver it to Mars too.

"*So, the answer to your question is,*
I do all of these on the **people's 'Faith on God'.**"

Thank You For Reading!

Thank you for reading my book.
I hope it brought a smile to your face and some
insights.
Please leave your feedback wherever you purchased
this book. Keep rocking!